This Little Tiger book belongs to:

_____

_____

_____

Ar gyfer Jude. Gyda fy
nymuniadau gorau, diolch - J L

LITTLE TIGER
An imprint of Little Tiger Press Limited
1 Coda Studios, 189 Munster Road,
London SW6 6AW
Imported into the EEA by
Penguin Random House Ireland,
Morrison Chambers, 32 Nassau Street,
Dublin D02 YH68
www.littletiger.co.uk

First published in France 2018
This edition published in Great Britain 2020

Text and illustrations copyright © Jonny Lambert 2018
Jonny Lambert has asserted his right to be identified
as the author and illustrator of this work
under the Copyright, Designs and Patents Act, 1988
A CIP catalogue record for this book is available
from the British Library

THE BIG ANGRY ROAR

Jonny Lambert

LITTLE TIGER

LONDON

As the pride patrolled,
the lion cubs squabbled.

First a push,

then a tumble,

followed by an "OW!"

"Stop it, you two!
Cub, don't hurt your
sister. You're old
enough to know better!"

"But she started it!"
snapped Cub.

And off he stomped.

"I'm so angry," scowled Cub.
"I think I might **pop!**"

"Popping won't help!" giggled Gnu.
"And it's terribly messy!" Zebra
sniggered. "Listen, Cub, you
have to learn to let your
anger out."

"When we're angry, we **tramp** and **stamp**

and

STOMP!"

Cub stamp-stomped up and down.

"Ouch! That hurt!" he angrily yelped.
"I stood on a stone. Stomping is stupid!"

Nursing a sore paw, Cub stormed off.

"I'm really angry now!" he shouted.

And he huffed and puffed and grumped!

"Oh, do stop with the boohoo!" snorted Rhino.

"You should do what we do," said Hippo.

"When we're annoyed . . ."

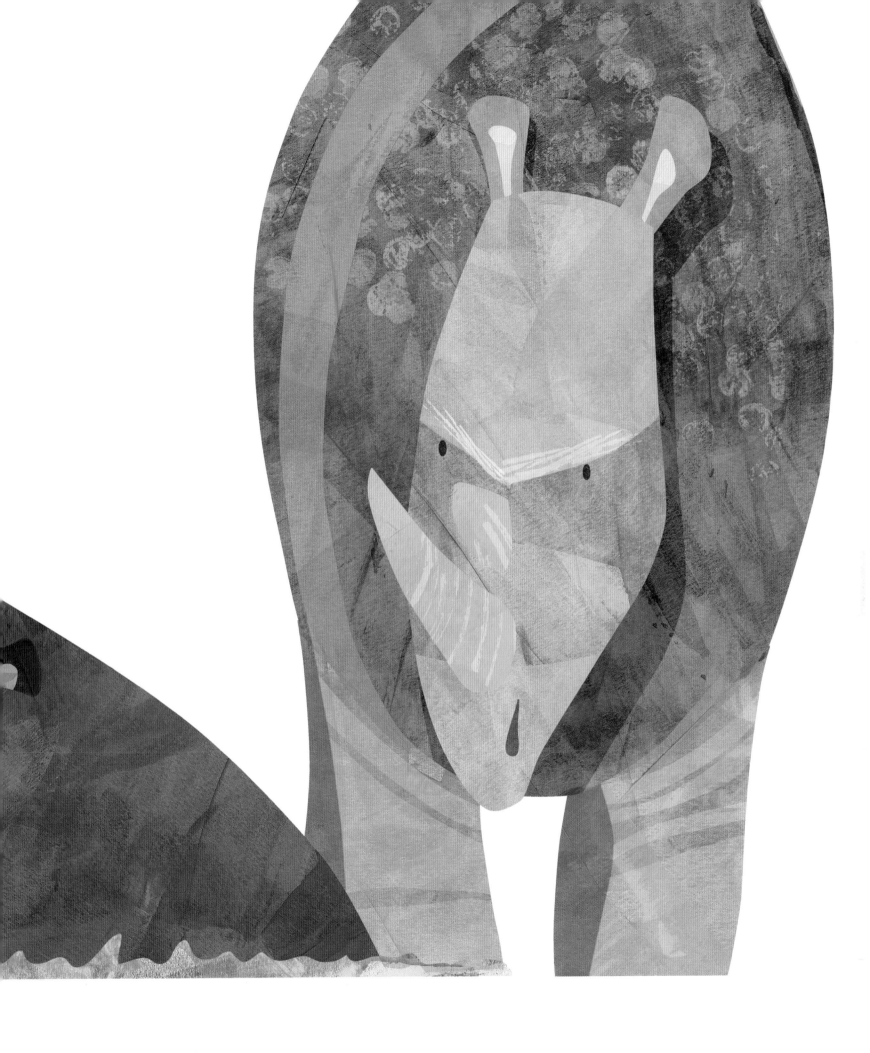

"...we

bash

and

crash,

splatter and splash!"

Cub charged up and down.

"Yuk! Now I'm smelly!" he bawled.

"Squelching and squishing is silly!"

Sulking and stinky, Cub clomped on . . .

SMACK!

. . . straight into Elephant's bottom.

"Hey, you're in my way!" shouted Cub.

"TOOT!" trumpeted Elephant crossly.

"ROAR!" growled Cub angrily.

TOOT! TOOT!

ROAR!

ROAR!

And they started
a massive . . .

STA

MPEDE!

"Oh no!" squeaked Cub.
"Did . . . did we do that?"
Baboon nodded.
He'd seen it all before.

"Everyone gets angry," smiled Baboon. "I do too. But I know how to let the anger out. Would you like to have a go?

First, breathe deeply in and out, and slowly count to ten."

"Pull lots of funny faces,

then start all over again!"

"I feel so much better," chuckled Cub.
"And my anger's gone. But I do
have something special to say . . ."

"Sorry."